Whiffy Wilson

the wolf who wouldn't go to bed.

For Judy and all the Devon Dumplings, with love – C.H

For Mimi and Daisy – L.L

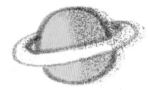

ORCHARD BOOKS

First published in Great Britain in 2015 by The Watts Publishing Group
This edition first published in 2016

1 3 5 7 9 10 8 6 4 2

Text © Caryl Hart, 2015
Illustrations © Leonie Lord, 2015

A CIP catalogue record for this book is available from the British Library.

ISBN 978 1 40833 255 9

Printed and bound in China

MIX
Paper from
responsible sources
FSC® C104740
FSC
www.fsc.org

Orchard Books
An imprint of Hachette Children's Group
Part of The Watts Publishing Group Limited
Carmelite House
50 Victoria Embankment
London EC4Y 0DZ

An Hachette UK Company
www.hachette.co.uk
www.hachettechildrens.co.uk

There was a wolf called Wilson
Who stayed up late at night.
He played with all his toys
Until the early morning light.

He practised on his saxophone,

He strummed his blue guitar.

Boom Boom

He sang and banged his big bass drum
Just like a superstar!

One night, while Whiffy Wilson
Was howling at the moon,
His best friend, Dotty, thundered round
And barged into his room.

"Wilson! Please be quiet!
You're making too much noise.
Why aren't you sleeping in your bed
Like other little boys?"

"BIG boys like me don't ever sleep,"
the cheeky wolf cub said.
"I've got important jobs to do.
I can't waste time in bed!"

"I need to line up all my cars,
And learn some magic tricks.

I have to build a giant fort,
And stack up all these bricks!"

Dotty made her friend sit down.
"Oh, Wilson, don't you know?
We need to sleep all through the night
To help our bodies grow.
Sleeping keeps us healthy.
It makes us strong and clever."

"Well, I'm not tired," Wilson yawned.
"I'll stay awake for ever."

"You silly thing," laughed Dotty.
"I can tell you need a rest.
I'll show you how, and soon you'll see
That bedtimes are the best."

"First we're going to tidy up –
I'll race you. Come on, quick!"

"I've won! I've won!" cried Wilson,
As he grabbed the final brick.

"Next, we'll have a bedtime feast
With toast and milk and honey."
Wilson wolfed it down and grinned,
"Thanks, Dotty, that was yummy!"

They made a cosy bedtime den,
Then Wilson had a bath.

He made a beard of bubbles.
"Hey! Look at me!" he laughed.

Dotty helped him brush his teeth
Until they shone and gleamed.

She dressed him in pyjamas,
"They're so cosy,"
Wilson beamed.

Dotty gave her friend a hug,
"It's story time," she said.

"So go and find your teddy bear,
Then hop straight into bed."

They read a tale of pirates,
And a book about a knight.
They found out how to train a dog,
And how to fly a kite!

Soon, Wilson's eyes were drooping,
And Dotty kept on yawning.
"Time to snuggle down," she said.
"I'll see you in the morning."

Then, Dotty switched the light off,
And she tucked the covers tight.
She turned the glowing
    nightlight on
And kissed her friend
    goodnight.

"This bedtime has been fun," he smiled,
"And not the least bit boring."
Then Whiffy Wilson closed his eyes
And very soon . . .

. . . was snoring!

He dreamed he was an astronaut,
Cruising through the stars.
He met a group of aliens
All driving hover cars!

They had an astro picnic
On a planet far away.

Then **ZOOM!**
went Wilson's rocket,
Round and round the Milky Way.

Next morning, Whiffy Wilson woke
And tumbled out of bed.
"I must thank Dotty straight away,
Last night was GREAT," he said.

Dotty opened up her door,
And rubbed her sleepy eyes.

"Good morning," whispered Wilson.
"I've brought you a surprise!
I had a lovely bedtime
And I slept the whole night through . . .

. . . so I've made a wolf-sized breakfast treat
Especially for you!"

the end.